LITTLE MISS CHATTERBOX

by Roger Hargreaves

Grosset & Dunlap
An Imprint of Penguin Random House

Little Miss Chatterbox talked more than a lot.

She talked all the time.

Day in and day out, week after week, month after month, year in and year out!

She never stopped!

She didn't know it, but she even talked in her sleep!

She had a brother.

I bet you can guess what his name was!

Can't you?

That's right!

Mr. Chatterbox!

She looks a bit like him, don't you think?

You should have heard them when they got together!

You couldn't get a word in edgeways.

Or sideways.

Or anyways!

Have you ever heard about somebody being able to talk the hind leg off a donkey?

Well, Mr. Chatterbox could talk both hind legs off a donkey.

And his sister could talk the hind leg off an elephant!

Now, this story is about the time Little Miss Chatterbox decided to get herself a job.

Which she did.

In a bank.

In Happyland.

At ten o'clock one Monday morning, Mr. Happy strolled into the HappyToLendYouBank in the middle of Happytown.

He took out his checkbook, wrote a check, and went to the counter.

Behind the counter, on her first morning at work, stood Little Miss Chatterbox.

She smiled at Mr. Happy.

Mr. Happy smiled back.

"Good morning," he said, cheerfully.

"Well," said Little Miss Chatterbox, taking a deep breath…

"For the time of the year it is a good morning but not as good as the morning we had yesterday and I dare say tomorrow morning will be an even better morning but it's quite a good morning for a Monday morning and…"

And she went on and on and on until it was time for the bank to close.

Mr. Happy was still standing there, with his mouth open in amazement.

He'd been there for hours!

"And now," continued Little Miss Chatterbox, "it's time for the bank to close and time for me to go home so good-bye and nice talking to you and…"

And she went home, leaving poor Mr. Happy without any money.

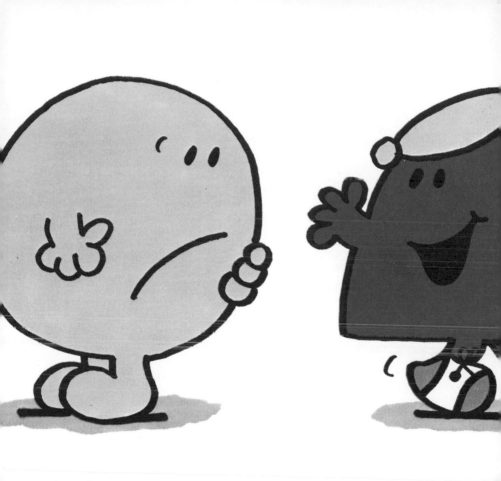

The following morning she was fired!

She got herself another job.

In a restaurant.

The Eatalot!

It was Tuesday morning, and at noon Mr. Greedy walked into the restaurant and sat himself down at his usual corner table.

He always ate there on Tuesdays because that was the day they served extra large portions.

The waitress came up to take his order.

"What's the soup of the day?" Mr. Greedy asked the waitress.

"Well," said Little Miss Chatterbox—for she was the waitress—"the soup of the day is tomato but we also have other soups on the menu such as oxtail and vegetable and chicken and chicken noodle but we have lots of other things to start with such as…"

And she went on and on and on.

Until midnight!

Mr. Greedy was still sitting there, listening, in amazement.

He'd been there for twelve hours!

Listening!

"And now," continued Little Miss Chatterbox, "it's time for the Eatalot Restaurant to close and for me to go home so good-bye and nice talking to you and…"

And she went home, leaving poor Mr. Greedy feeling rather empty.

The next morning she was fired!

The same thing happened all week long.

On Thursday morning she was fired from her job as an assistant in a hat shop.

Miss Splendid went into the shop to buy herself a new hat, but she couldn't!

"Oh Madam I've just the hat for you and I know you're going to love it because it's pink and pink is your color and it…"

It was all talk, and no hat!

On Friday morning she was fired from her job as a secretary to Mr. Uppity.

Mr. Uppity, incidentally, was the richest man in the world!

I just thought you'd like to know.

But poor Mr. Uppity didn't make any money the day that Little Miss Chatterbox was working for him.

Oh, no!

"Oh Mr. Uppity I've never worked in an office before and isn't it exciting and would you like a cup of coffee and are you as rich as everybody says you are and it…"

It was all talk and no work!

But, this story has a happy ending because at the very end of that week Little Miss Chatterbox managed to find herself a job that suited her down to the ground.

And up to the sky!

That Saturday evening Mr. Chatterbox was at home in Chatterbox Cottage.

Which was where he lived.

Mr. Chatterbox was mad because his watch had stopped and he had arranged to meet Little Miss Sunshine at seven o'clock and he had no idea what the time was.

So, he decided to call the Time to find out what time it was.

He dialed the number.

"…at the tone the time will be six twenty-five and fifteen seconds!"

Little Miss Chatterbox took a deep breath.

BEEP!

"At the tone the time will be six twenty-five and twenty seconds!"

BEEP!

"That's funny," thought Mr. Chatterbox to himself. "That sounds just like my sister!"